The Five Hole Stories

Dave Bidini

BRINDLE
& GLASS

Library and Archives Canada Cataloguing in Publication
Bidini, Dave
The five hole stories / Dave Bidini.

ISBN 1-897142-18-8

1. Erotic stories, Canadian (English). 2. Hockey stories, Canadian (English). I. Title.

PS8603.I34F59 2006   C813'.6   C2006-905087-2

Cover and interior images: Matt James
Author photo: David Wiewel

 Canada Council   Conseil des Arts
for the Arts   du Canada

Brindle & Glass is pleased to thank the Canada Council
for the Arts and the Alberta Foundation for the Arts for their
contributions to our publishing program.

Brindle & Glass Publishing
www.brindleandglass.com

1   2   3   4   5   09   08   07   06

PRINTED AND BOUND IN CANADA

For Beddoes, Frayne, Shakey and the rest,
and to Bill Chahley

And now it is time to call attention
to our bed, a forest of skin
where seeds burst like bullets.

Anne Sexton
"Now"

CONTENTS

ONE HUNDRED BUCKS

Dolores hung around whenever the Leafs visited Chicago. It was her thing. Those were tough times, and people had to pick up dough here and there, wherever they could. The Eagle was your typical post-game watering hole. It was the kind of place that doesn't exist anymore. These days, it's all private clubs and hotel suites and swank condos that players swap with each other. But at the Eagle, you'd wait until after the game had ended and the visiting team had settled in, then you'd go up to guys like Ulcers MacCool, the goaltender, and tell him what for, how you hadn't paid two bucks just to see some overweight geezer stone the host team. MacCool would call you a putz and then drink the drink you bought for him, and sometimes, if he didn't like what he saw, he'd ask, "So where's the sirloin tonight?" and you'd tell him what you knew, which wasn't much, because you were married and had no idea how to score, at least not at that time of the night. Not that it mattered to those guys, being married. They were all rogues out there on the road, getting paid crap and being yelled at half the day, but also living a dream that included a bit of action whenever there was something new and fresh at the Eagle, or when some sap like me had a sister, and not an ounce of respect for her.

But Eddie Burns I liked, and if I'd had a sister, I might've helped him out. Eddie was a decent guy. Unlike a lot of players, he didn't make you feel like some kinda pathetic garden worm. Eddie would let you finish your thought, raise his head, wink, and say: "Listen, all this good talk is making me thirsty. You?" It was the signal that it was your turn to buy—christ, it was always your turn to buy—but you did it because Eddie was an NHLer and you had to pay for the privilege. Some of them I didn't have time for, but not Eddie Burns. He'd tell you flat out who was pulling their weight and who wasn't, and unlike a lot of players, Eddie knew how to tell a story that had a beginning, middle and end. It came naturally. He was a deep thinker, even though he was missing teeth and had a voice like a cement truck. Were Eddie an actor, he might have been John Garfield, maybe Bogie: someone who'd been slugged black by life, but had fought back with paint cans.

When Eddie Burns first noticed Dolores, it

was the end of you or I sitting down with him and talking turkey. He had less time for hangers-on like myself, even though I was more than that. Christ, I was a walking hockey encyclopedia, intimately involved with the game. I was useful to the right player, provided he wasn't only thinking with his dick. That's why it was hard to accept the fact that Eddie was no longer interested in letting me bend his ear. It was hard to swallow. For most of the '48 season, he and Dolores met at the Eagle whenever the Leafs came to town, which was often. They'd take a small nook in the far corner of the bar and talk all night, sinking deeper into each other's lives before heading back to their own fleabag digs and ruminating on the tightrope of love and the possibility of hope and the inevitable pain and misery that they knew laid in wait for them.

Nobody had seen this coming. Dolores was pretty much everybody's girl. I'd seen her leave with other players loads of times: musicians, band leaders, and the odd actor, too, sometimes even a big-shot producer who was passing through ChiTown mounting a show. There were a few girls like Dolores around, but like I said, this was a time when nobody had anything extra to their name. You picked up cash wherever you could. It wasn't a case of being lawless or loose. Working on the side was as much about frugality and hard work as anything else. Me, I did all kinds of jobs—not the same activities as Dolores, mind you—but sure, I ran the odd number, delivered the odd nefarious package for scratch. Everybody was reaching for the same bar, fumbling around trying to hike up to the next level, past steerage or abject poverty. There was only so much space, and you had to get yours, at whatever cost. Dolores was part of that. I was part of that. We were a culture of sloppy-footed climbers, by hick or by friggin' crick.

The first words that Eddie said to Dolores were, "I've seen you here before, haven't I?" Dolores thought it was a joke, because nobody had ever used such an obvious line on her. Mostly it was just, "Hey, toots. Fancy this?" or "A sawbuck says there's some sugar for me under that petticoat." Besides, this large, hurt-faced man must have known at least a handful of her previous dates. Half of them were probably even Leafs themselves. There's just no way that Eddie was blind to her reputation. Unless he'd made himself blind. Which a man will do.

"Sorry. You must be confusing me with a certain Queen of England," she told Eddie, flat-out. "See, the old dame comes in here all the time."

Eddie thought that Dolores's voice was as soft and lovely as the batting of a robin's wing. Love will do that to you, because the truth is, her timbre had been roughed up working the counter at Leone's, slinging plates and pinch-hitting whenever the dishwasher was too drunk to sop. Her brother's kid was a cripple, too, and she helped out with that, passing tip money on to him when she was flush. She didn't like being a waitress—who did?—but she kept the gig because it gave her a normal life beyond the moonlighting. Well, not normal. Nobody had a normal life in those days. We didn't have the suburbs, hot wax, cable television, insta-bank, psychoanalysis, whatever. We took our shots, and gave the world a piece. It wasn't only Dolores's voice that had been ground down from the vagaries of the world, but her hands and fingers, too—not to mention the heels and arches of her feet, and the small of her back, which burned like a hot plate on Sundays, holidays and whenever the temperature dipped below freezing.

"Maybe it's your hair. Did you change it?" he insisted.

"Forty degrees of Sandra Dee," she said, pushing up curls that curved off her cheeks like treble clefs. "Otherwise, it's SNAFU, if you get my drift."

"Well, it looks fine now. Fine."

"You should see it after a shift at the delicatessen. You've heard of Medusa?"

"I can't imagine. Not the way it looks here."

"I guess I better just shut up then, and take the compliment."

"Yes. You better."

"To tell the truth, my humility needs a good grease job. Seven and seven, if you please."

Dolores excused herself to the powder room, and when she came back, Eddie had grabbed a booth for the two of them. He brushed off the rest of us like dandruff, explaining nothing. I could accept it, sure, but it was strange to see this powerful man so overwhelmed by the moment. You could tell that Dolores took Eddie for a mug, with his brush cut, punched-up nose and enormous hands. His hands were the first thing anyone noticed, the kind of hands that only nature can create—but the closer she studied

Eddie's face, the less it looked like a clawed-over prairie field, and the more it looked like a series of soft folds and rumpled bedsheets, gathered wool that had knotted and woven into itself over time.

Eddie kept his distance in the beginning. But with only six teams in the league, he was back in ChiTown a lot. While he was away, he sent Dolores flowers, had chocolates delivered to her at work. He even sprung for a singing telegram on her birthday. The messenger was a pock-marked shrimp in a duck tail and tux, but everyone at Leone's agreed he could sing. It was schmaltzy stuff, sure, but no one had ever come within a country mile of doing these kinds of things for Dolores. In fact, it was usually the opposite routine—ten bucks crumpled in a ball on the night table, a half sack of gin, a pack of Buckinghams, some scented soap or nylons if she was lucky. And even though she continued to hit the Eagle, picking up scratch here and there to supplement her measly diner's wage, she started to feel as if maybe Eddie's infatuation with her was real and true and decent, and that, of all of those impossible scenarios where love is the conquering force over misery and loneliness and sadness, perhaps she was living a dream that was real and good from which she was not required to wake up.

Mid-season, they finally got together. It happened after a long walk along Lake Huron on the good side of March. Eddie was wearing a time-beaten houndstooth jacket; Dolores was dressed in a red coat with a puff-fringed hood and tassels.

"What's it been, three months?" asked Eddie.

"What's what been?" replied Dolores, smoking.

"Don't be coy, my little bird."

"Little bird? I'm your American eagle. And you're my Canada goose. Honking and making a racket, right here in the middle of the street."

"I'm not the one stopping traffic."

"Puh-leaze."

"I speak the truth."

"It's my fatal flaw," she said, taking Eddie's hand. "I always think people are giving me the business, even when they're not. Why do you think that is?"

"I like it that you don't take things too seriously."

"I'm not a comedienne, you know."

"I know."

"If I were funny, I'd be opening for Mel Torme."

"If you were opening for Mel Torme, you wouldn't be here."

"Vegas, Atlantic City. The lights, the rabble . . ."

"What's Mel Torme got that I don't?"

"Money, brains, a nose that doesn't look like it's sparred with a shovel . . ."

"I'll give you that."

". . . and probably a nicer coat, too."

"I know what he doesn't have."

They walked another ten steps in silence, and then Dolores turned to Eddie, giving him the whole of her face.

"Say it anyway," she said.

"You. He doesn't have you."

They went to the Embassy Hotel. With the wind sighing like a low trombone against the quick drumming of the city, they pulled each other down. Dolores felt the whole of her lover's body: the stab of his shoulder and crook of his hip, his rippling neck and patch of stubble between his ear and cheek, the roll of his stomach, river of fingers, nervous knees and wonky feet, and down there, the pug of his shaft, which, as they fell on the bed, drove against her like an apple into the loam. The bedside lamp buzzed, but otherwise, the silence was like singing. Dolores breathed hot against Eddie's face as his brow drove against hers, hiding quick tongues that darted like violin bows in the black.

Dolores's body was milky white, with no shadow of a tan. Back in those days, nobody got much sunlight, even in the summer; it seemed that people were too busy working and sleeping and working some more to make time for good weather. As Eddie cupped the fullness of her breasts, he hoped she'd ignore the roughness of his hands, which had ten years of faceoffs and hack fights and train rides carved into them. Eddie dragged his tongue up Doe's neck like a deer licking a tree, then gummed the curve of her jaw while moving his other hand to her ass, which writhed against the bedspread and, further down, grew wet with the moment. Dolores wriggled out of her bra straps and freed her hands, palming Eddie's back. His body was hot, his shoulder blades moving in a pinching motion like two wings working the air. Eddie held himself up on his forearms and moved into her. While

they made love, she felt the raw strength of his
body, but it was the softness of his abdomen and
the touch of his sac flinging against her that made
it feel like a tender act, as if their bodies were at
play. But it was fucking all the same, a see-sawing
of bones and sinew, a fatty press of heat. When
she finally opened her eyes, a string of spittle
hung from his lip as his eyes slanted in ecstasy,
his brow sharply furrowed. As Eddie moved to
climax, Doe brought her hands to his ass and
pulled him closer—harder—against her, hitting
the button. Her hair whipped side to side against
the sheets as the bedsprings sawed like wheezing
harmonicas, and, as if in a dream, she heard
the melancholy of moaning trumpets and crying
guitars and sad small pianos, and pretty soon, all
that was ever red became blue, and the plume of
smoke from their bed rose and licked the ceiling
and was gone.

• • •

Jock McIlhargey, The Scotsman, was Eddie's
rival. Their style of hockey was close—as grace-
ful and weightless as it was incendiary and violent—but their appearance was not. If Eddie's face

possessed a softness despite its jagged carvings, The Scotsman's mug was like uncracked alabaster. He had a great white forehead that suggested the cold flat face of a hammer. Had the rest of his body not been built like a Brink's truck, his head would have appeared impossibly large and weighted. But if you weren't daunted by his size, The Scotsman had deep dark caverns for eyes. It was what they didn't show you that made you step away.

I never cared for McIlhargey as a person. Whenever he hit the Eagle—which wasn't as often as his less distinguished teammates—newbies chased the hem of his coat like hounds after a tailpipe. But McIlhargey never looked like he fit into the scenery. He was often crowded by an entourage that I swore he'd assembled from one of the local peanut gangs, and you never knew when any number of them might have been packing. As a result, his time at the Eagle was always more show than bullrap. The few times that I tried to get into it with him, he arrowed his eyes at me suspiciously, drew me into his long caverns, and wanted to know where a mook like me got off grilling him about Taffy's ankle or how come he couldn't beat Gainsworth of Montreal. I was always in a tough spot regarding whether or not to cheer for The Scotsman. True, he was standoffish and arrogant, but he was also the only Blackhawk player with the ability to bring glory to our championship-mad town. Among the game's *cognoscenti*, he was worshipped like no other hockey player in the dives, beer cellars and rat-bitten taverns of our burg—to say nothing of the gilded ballrooms and champagne hallways of the Upper West Side where debutantes and dukes treated him to tall women, long cigars and fine spirits.

• • •

In the hot, early spring of '48, Toronto settled in to face Chicago in a five gamer to decide which team would advance to the final against Montreal. During the regular season, Eddie, long smooched by the dove of love, skated as if buttering a cloud. He captained the Leafs' attack and led his team in scoring. Pundits whispered that the Hart Trophy would be his by season's end, at least when they weren't whispering about how this right winger and that D-man had bedded Eddie's dove back in '46, and how they'd helped her by showing her what to do with her hands when all they'd required was her mouth. Once, after losing myself in too many White Russians, I got up the nerve to ask Eddie's linemate, Legs Rooney, if Burnsie had heard from any of the league's goons regarding his tryst. Rooney, looking both ways over his shoulder, told me that Eddie heard it, but that the lovestruck gomer treated the gossip and trash talk as if it were so much romantic poetry, plucking out Doe's name like a glimmering pearl in the muck and using it as motivation to batter his opponent better than the league had seen in twenty years.

Dolores, for her part, wore her happiness like a wreath. She baubled and belled through the streets, a chevron of light in the dirty thoroughfares and hard roads of the city. The open-shoed rummies who came into Leone's looking for a ten-cent cup of coffee were treated to the folly of her smile as she slung hash and home fries along the counter. The old joint sang with life despite the misery of the walking masses, and when you stood across the street staring in, it was like a dazzling hive to which the city's wandering drones were drawn.

When Doe wasn't at work, she was sitting in her tenement apartment painting her nails or reading a penny novel. On other occasions, she'd wander the park and pore over one of Eddie's missives by the lamplight—which, back in the day, illuminated the lakeshore like a thousand matchsticks. In his letters, Eddie wrote a little about the team, but mostly he told stories of Hogtown: brunch at the Ford Hotel, fancy-dress evenings at the Royal York, Sunnyside pool, a trolley ride to the bluffs, the maze of canals around Toronto Island, the smokies at Maple Leaf Stadium, trout fishing on the Credit River, and the new city park—High Park—where foxes, coyotes, and swans played in a cradle of natural life. After Doe had studied the details of the stationery—the blots of blue that dabbed the edge of the paper, their small, tight words scribbled by a balled-up hand arthritic at the wrist—she folded the letter and slipped it in her purse, then pushed the purse under her arm, wandering through the sparkling city as if harbouring the diamond blue.

One night after work, Doe hit the town with a friend, Rose, who over shandies and ciders asked if she ever suspected Eddie of carrying on with a Doe or two in another NHL city.

"The notion never crossed my mind," she told her.

"These things have to be considered, dearie, what with all the travel these fellows do."

"I know, but Eddie's different. Don't give me that look," she said, wagging a finger at Rose.

"If anyone should see it, Doe, it should be you."

"With Eddie, I haven't a doubt in the world," she said, pushing up her treble clefs.

"Well, you know what they say about love being blind."

"Rose, he writes me letters. I've never known a man who could write his name, let alone put his thoughts to paper."

"I guess the Eagle must be pretty quiet these days without the likes of you," said Rose.

"I suppose it is."

"You don't go at all?"

"I did for a while, but not anymore. Truthfully, I kind of miss the rabble. But I treasure my times alone with the big oaf, too, you know."

"We should just duck in," said Rose.

"You go. I've seen enough of that place."

"But now you can go there on your own terms. You don't have to hustle anymore. You're a kept woman, girlie."

"You in the marketplace or something?"

"Honey, I'm always in the marketplace," said Rose, pushing together her breasts.

After finishing their drinks, Doe consented to a one last visit to the Eagle. There was a lineup outside, and when Doe groused about it being too long, Rose told her to stuff the nonsense: if anyone had earned a free pass, it was her. The doorman took one look at Doe, shouted, "Cleopatra returns in triumph!" and ushered the young women through the door.

The bar was packed, as usual. I spotted Doe the minute she walked in. For some reason, she looked as tall and elegant as an oak tree, even though I'd never thought of her as being tall before. Doe and Rose took a booth near the back of the room and ordered drinks, which the barkeep insisted on buying. They were well into it by the time The Scotsman approached them. Rose spritzed her neck with perfume as the tall centreman stood at their booth, leaned in with slow menace, and placed his palms flat on the tabletop.

"Some night to be working, eh, girls?" he grinned.

"Actually, we're off the payroll," said Rose. "So long as our luck holds, anyway," she said, tapping the wood.

"Haven't I seen you here before?" The Scotsman asked Doe, echoing Eddie's first words.

"I've graduated," said Doe, throwing up her hands. "I'm strictly varsity this year."

"Nice to see that good kids can still get ahead in this world," said Jock, taking his fedora into his hands.

"Hey, you're good to people, they're good to you. And I mean 'gooood'," said Doe, elbowing Rose, who snorkelled a laugh.

"Is that so?"

"That," said Doe, stabbing the air drunkenly, "is . . . so!"

"And what do you do, stranger?" Rose asked The Scotsman.

"I play the game of hockey. Pretty darned well if you asked half the people in this bar," he boasted.

"My boyfriend plays hockey. Pretty darned well, as well," said Doe.

"Might I have heard of him?" asked The Scotsman.

"Yup. Eddie Burns," said Doe, nodding her head.

"Schlong out to here," said Rose, measuring

the air. Doe barked, then covered her mouth with her hands.

"Well, you know what they say about hockey players," The Scotsman told them, leaning in so that his eyes became hooded in shadow.

Tippled and loose, Rose and Doe made room for Jock. After about an hour of repartee, the three strangers found themselves walking back to Rose's apartment, bound for a bottle of Maker's Mark. Someone cracked the hooch and Doe found a bandstand program on the radio. Within moments, the two women were spinning each other around the carpet while the hockey star watched from a chair. After their fifth or sixth dance, they collapsed on the divan. The Scotsman rose from his seat, slipped a hand inside his vest, and took out his billfold.

"Ladies," he said, clearing his throat. "A proposition."

"I'm a kept woman!" said Doe, shooting a finger into the air and laughing.

"Yeah, and I'm . . ." said Rose. "Wait a minute. Do what you will with me, hockey star!" said Rose, throwing her hand to her forehead.

"No, it ain't like that," said Jock. "See, this here is a hundred-dollar bill," he said, pulling out the C-note and snapping it with both hands.

"Jesus, Mary and Joseph," said Doe, awestruck.

"One hundred bucks," said The Scotsman.

These days, a hundred bucks is something you might find in the coin slot of a payphone. But in 1948, it was five months' pay, a nub of gold bullion, box seats at the Met, a train trip to San Francisco, a suite at the Bismark. The bill itself was a work of art, something you saw only once, maybe twice, in your life, like the Mona Lisa or the Brothers DiMaggio. Held in front of Dot and Rose, it possessed a rare power, and as The Scotsman waved it, both women knew that it was a moment they'd remember, and talk about, for the rest of their lives.

"What's the hitch?" said Doe, snapping out of her reverie.

"Depending on how you look at things, there's no hitch at all," said McIlhargey.

"There's always a hitch," said Doe. "I didn't fall backwards out of a turnip truck, Mr. Blackhawk."

"All I want," said McIlhargey, "is to watch you girls for a while."

"Watch us? Well, take a good look, handsome,"

said Rose, teasing the bottom of her skirt.

"Just fool around a little for me," he said, pointing his finger and twirling it.

"Fool around? You mean like this?" said Rose, pinching Doe in the ribs, making her whoop with surprise.

"Over there, like," said The Scotsman, gesturing to the bed that sat in the corner of the room.

"Oh, the picture is becoming clearer now," said Doe.

"You can start with a little kissing," he sneered.

"You sure that hunny's real, soldier?" asked Rose. "Let me touch it if it is."

The Scotsman handed her the C-note.

"Doe, Jesus . . ." said Rose. But Eddie Burns's girl had already unbuttoned her shirt and was patting the bed. "Rose, it's not every day that a coupla floozies like us run into the likes of Abe Lincoln over there," she said, her thoughts turning to what her share of the payload would fetch: a wedding gown, a pewter money clip for her dent-faced mook, a train trip north to the land of the caribou, some coin for her brother and a day at the city zoo with her nephew, a

Christmas token for Old Man Leone's family, a pair of loafers, a jar of peppermint sticks, six months at the bijou, a glass of absinthe, an armful of glossy magazines . . .

"Rose, come here," said Doe, draining her glass and falling backwards.

• • •

When Eddie arrived at Houseman Station for game five of the Leafs' semi-final versus Chicago, he phoned Doe and told her that he had an hour free before practice. Doe told Eddie to meet her at Leone's. When he arrived, he found the place crackling with life. As he made his way through a press of long coats and wool jackets, Old Man Leone spotted him first. He clapped his hands: "Mr. Eddie Burns! An enemy to the Hawks, but a friend of Leones!" Doe was working a table at the back of the room, and she spun on her heels. She came forward and lost her hands in Eddie's, then leaned over and pecked him on the cheek.

"This is one helluva tough crowd, eh, Doe?" whispered Eddie.

"Watch it, fella. These folks'll turn on ya in a heartbeat," she said, snapping her fingers.

"Now: here!" said Mr. Leone, clearing away the best table in the joint. "Young man, sit!"

To Eddie, Doe looked like a million bucks. It went beyond the usual glow and sunshine. Her face was dusted with rouge, her eyes charcoal-drawn. Missing was the long day's perfume he'd come to desire; instead, when Eddie leaned in he smelled kiwi, pomegranate, coconut.

"Doe, your shoes," he said, as she crossed her legs out of the side of the booth.

"Like them? Eddie, the window at Bloomingdale's was calling to me. I believe the ancients call it an out-of-body experience."

"The last time I had one of those, I was chewing on Eddie Shore's hipbone."

"Certainly not as pleasant as chewing on a certain someone else's."

"Certainly not," said Eddie, loosening his tie.

"You look top rank, Eddie," said Doe, sipping her coffee.

"I was gonna say the same to you," he told her, raking his fingers through his hair. "I mean, it's really, really something, Doe, what with your shoes and all," he said, shaking his head.

"You sound surprised, sailor."

"No. Delighted is the word."

"Eddie, I don't believe we've ever spent this much time discussing footwear," said Doe. "Shouldn't we press on with more important matters?"

"Like what?" asked Eddie.

"Well, I couldn't possibly imagine," she sighed, laying her cheek on her hand.

Word of their engagement passed from booth to booth, and soon, everyone in the diner was congratulating them. Old Man Leone cried and wiped his eyes with the counter rag. He said they'd have the wedding right there in the restaurant. Eddie and Doe clung to each other like moths to lamplight, smooching on demand. Finally, when Rose showed up, decked out in a long elegant coat with silver-studded barrettes clipped across her hair, she pulled Eddie close and gave him the what-for, as if he were her own. Rose told him, "You're marrying the greatest gal in the world. All she's done for us, it's more than anyone should expect." Eddie thought that was pretty high praise for his little dove of a waitress, but then again, she was no ordinary dove.

• • •

THE FIVE HOLE

Doe walked to the rink with the rest of us. On Waverly Avenue, there were barkers waving bouquets of pennants—five cents a flag—and cotton candy. Peanut and chestnut vendors pushed at her elbow. Together we rumbled towards the newly bricked rink—mooks and millionaires side by side in a sea of excitement. You could tell the fellers and the Rockefellers apart by what we were wearing. Me, I favoured my old bomber jacket and boots, but the men from Barrington Heights and Oak Park wore wool coats and fedoras, their wives showing off white gloves and heels that clacked against the road like rows of chattering teeth. These people were like glittering tiles in the ChiTown mosaic. They'd withstood the hammering of our times, their lifestyles supported by a bedrock of foundry dividends, estate living, and an entitlement of old money channelled through the bulge of midwestern industry. Their parents and grandparents had watched over the rise of the city's blooming stonescape, and it was now theirs to enjoy. Occasionally, you'd hear a word you'd never heard before rise up from them like a coloured balloon—"concierge," "splendiferous," "corollary"—making someone like Doe feel as if she were playing a minor role in a great swirling novel by Thackeray or Flaubert or some other writer whose name had been borrowed by a nylon stocking manufacturer or cigarette company to give their stock a mark of distinction. Still, Doe relished the fact that she was the lone scurrying figure in the crowd whose dent-headed husband-to-be would decide whether or not these couples remained lip-locked on their cab ride home after the game or subdued and lost in the smog of defeat. As she approached the face of the building, she drew a ten spot of The Scotsman's money from her purse and bought a ticket from a glass-eyed tout standing in front of the rink. Falling away from the moneyed crowd, who filed through the bright front doors of the rink into its glowing atrium, she peeled off with the rest of us for that long rafter climb into the smoky corners of the rink.

• • •

In the depths of Chicago Stadium, Eddie felt as if he were sitting in the mouth of a whale, a great moaning sound droning from beyond the dressing room door. Eddie could see that some of the kids looked as if they were about to parachute over the Black Forest, so he steadied them by raising his stick, passing a finger underneath the blade, then rising to let his equipment settle on his shoulders, his great, unshaking hands and body weighted with a sense of calm determination as he stood in front of his stall and announced: "Tonight. Tonight is our night, boys." Everybody exhaled as Eddie moved toward the door.

Under the hot arena lamps, the rink shook with life. Touts had sold blank-faced tickets to patrons who paid for the right to stand on ladder rungs behind the end blues. In the high corners of the rink, young fans wound themselves into the struts, where they watched the game like spiders from their webbing. The cheap seats were a mass of rage and vitriol. People drank, swore, brawled. During the game, they lit hot pennies and screws and bolts and tossed them to the ice. They chewed on Bavarian sausage and swilled whiskey and waved their fists with the see-saw drama of the action. Those sweet-faced, shower-gelled, martini-drinkers you see sitting in the fancy seats at today's games? They wouldn't have got through the concourse of the arena. They would have been like porterhouse to the snarling lions.

For the beginning of the series, The Scotsman

held his cards for as long as he had to. The Hawks had taken the first two games of the series, but the Leafs won back-to-back games at home, and as the stand-off returned to Chicago, it was all about which team had the strongest will and the fiercest heart.

It wasn't until the two minute mark of the third period—score tied 1–1—that The Scotsman surprised Eddie Burns. After struggling for the puck along the boards, Jock bumped Eddie with his shoulder as the play died and asked him: "How's that little tart of yours, Ed? She planning to wear white to the wedding?"

Eddie steeled himself and skated away. But a shift later in the faceoff circle, The Scotsman continued talking: "You know what they say about those Eaglewood dollies, dontcha? Could suck a titmouse through a tailpipe."

Eddie showed The Scotsman his daggers.

"Remember, boyo, I play hockey in this here town. I've got a read on all the best action."

Eddie stepped out of the faceoff circle, but was called back in. The referee told The Scotsman to quit his yapping and put his stick down.

"Fine, fine."

Eddie moved back into the circle. He tightened

his hands on his stick like a man trying to strangle a cat as the two players leaned into each other. Eddie could feel The Scotsman press his temple against his, then slide away as Eddie pressed back. The Scotsman grunted as he pushed in kind:

"Though I'd be remiss not to mention a certain birthmark."

The puck spanked off the ice. The Scotsman grabbed it and skated down the rink. Eddie followed until he could get close, then dug the blade of his stick into The Scotsman's ribs, pulling him to the ice and whispering through gritted teeth, "You mud-sucking piece of Glasgow trash." Jock rolled away, saying nothing. At the next faceoff, he spoke again.

"About four inches long, Burnsie. On the outside of her right thigh, I believe."

Eddie straightened up over the faceoff dot.

"Who told you?"

"Nobody told me, sap," said The Scotsman.

Eddie moved in slow murder towards McIlhargey. For a moment, his rumpled bedsheet skin hardened as the ref brought his hands to the centreman's chest: "Get a hold of yourself, Eddie."

"You take me for someone who'd stand back and let every two-bit mucker have a piece of that kind of derelict ass?" said Jock. "She's had every player in this league. She'll fuck anyone for money."

Eddie felt sick in the pit of his stomach. His heart hurt and his eyes stung as he reached for The Scotsman's throat. In the time it takes a matchstick to light and lick the air, the players on both teams knew what was happening. Reacting to their captain's anger, each Leaf grabbed a Blackhawk until the ice was a twisting mass of wool, steel and leather. The home crowd beat their fists against the glass. Eddie could feel The Scotsman's heartbeat plugged at his throat, but still he pressed down with a sick blind rage. The Scotsman's knees buckled and he fought to breathe as Eddie drove him down, where his head hit the ice like a melon. Moving his hands from the groove of his opponent's flesh, Eddie stood up and searched for Doe in the stands. He wanted to read her eyes. He wanted to see her lovely pale moon of a face set against the awful raging red and black of the crowd. Eventually, he found her leaning over the railing and moaning that she had only tried to do right against the gathering sadness that haunted the dreams of the barely living. The cheap-seaters laid their rough hands on the little dove who sang Eddie's name and pulled her under. Eddie broke across the ice and drove into the crowd. Soon we were flat to the Earth, all of us.

WHY I LOVE WAYNE BRADLEY

The scene was the same as it had always been in the dressing room after the game: hockey players splayed naked getting rubbed down on a table in the middle of the room, the coach cramming numbers into little grids in his office, and over in the corner, just as I had seen a hundred times before, the greatest hockey player in the world sitting doe-eyed in front of his locker answering reporters' questions like a fourteen-year-old boy being noticed for the first time.

It was that innocence that I fell for.

It's how I came to love Wayne Bradley.

After the game, we'd go out—me, 77, Murph, maybe McSummerly—and pick up chicks, maybe do a little *schnay*, get shit-faced. At the end of the night, Wayne would carry me out of the bar, then load me into the backseat. I'd sit with my head on his lap and tell him: "Dammit, Wayne, fuck, you know that I love you."

"Ah, Squid, man, I love you too, brother," he'd say.

Back at the hotel, I dreamed that we lived

in a grassy shack near the ocean, spooning on a bamboo mat while toucans sang from the tall trees. Then I'd wake up and realize who I was—a good old pussy-hunting, red-blooded Canadian hockey player.

Boy, was I confused.

Watching the Gifted One get undressed—his bony white ribcage, lithe dancer's arms, Christmas-ham thighs and acorn-hanging-from-a-smoked-frank penis revealed under the cold arena lighting—I'd fantasize about the two of us walking through the streets of Blind River, parading in front of my friends, family, Aunt Hildy, Coach Billingsworth, my Grade Four teacher, Cherry Jesperson (who laughed at my Grade Ten penis before blithely popping it into her mouth), and the whole goddamned hockey populace. The butterfly goalie and the all-time all-star moving together in a total representation of male love, our passion cascading across the fag-hating frozen tundra like fireworks out of Harold Ballard's asshole.

Me and Wayne.

We'd tell the world.

The rest of the Oilers fucked women without any kind of social pretense. Once, I watched two Hall-of-Famers adjudicate a Best Breast competition in the back of Players's Nightclub in the Cincinnati Hilton. Bottle blondes in silk blouses and leather bustiers approached their table and unstrung their tops as the boys Sharpied a number from one to ten on their stomachs. The tens were rewarded later with a view from the thirtieth floor of a downtown hotel, while the rest spent the night pondering enhancement surgery and the ignominy of sleeping with a non-roster player still bunking with his aunt. My routine with the ladies wasn't much different. I'd procure my evening's plaything after a broad sexual tango meant to impress my teammates—coaxing the girl with the body like dripping molasses into a cab with promises of propulsive, beastly sex—only to spend the night mindlessly driving around whatever town we were in, letting her fondle me while I stared out at the buildings. Eventually, I'd tell her that my shoulder medication had left me soft, and that, if she wouldn't mind keeping word of these troubles to herself, I'd arrange platinum seats for her and a friend the next time the team swung through town. I'd arrive back at the hotel wearing a dizzied face, as if I'd just had my brains fucked out. My roommate at the time, The Chief, was forever impressed with tales of my sexual escapades.

"... and then she brought out the cocker spaniel, and things started to get really weird," I'd tell him.

"A dog? No fuckin' way!"

On the bus, my impossibly lurid sex life was the talk of the Oilers. I was a cock-waving hero to my teammates. Me, I could get a chick to do whatever I wanted.

As the season wore on, my relationship with Wayne grew tighter. We discovered different things to do on the road, going to concerts, movies, art galleries. When I first met him, he was really into his soda pop bottle collection, but after a while, I turned him on to other things, like Canadian poetry. It freaked me out to find that he'd posted an Earle Birney poem, "Way to the West," on the bulletin board in the dressing room prior to a road trip. That's when I began to yearn for him in limousines, bars, nightclubs, and hotel elevators, whenever he and I got drunk. "Wayne, I love you more than anything," I'd whisper as we nodded off through the booze. Sometimes, he'd pat my head or squeeze my bicep. I thought there might be a chance. A slim chance.

During the playoffs that year, we met Calgary in the first round. Game six went into double overtime. That night, we lost five players in a bench-clearing brawl. The games were vicious and bloody, the trainers pulling guys off the ice like the war dead. In the third period, a kid named Lacombe, who had a Pagliaro moustache and a face like a garbage truck, wailed on my glove after I'd trapped the puck. Coming to my defence, Wayne skated past and tripped him, knocking the thug to the ice.

Kept on a short leash by Calgary's coach— or, perhaps, aware that he was helpless against the forces of unspoken love—Lacombe pulled himself to his feet and skated away, spitting *fuckingpussyboyfaggot* to himself. But one period later, in overtime, The Gifted One and Lacombe became entangled in the corner. Fighting for a loose puck that had long since jitterbugged free, they fell together in a wiry mess, arms and legs bent under each other. Landing in a crush, Lacombe pinned Wayne flush to the ice, his stick flattened across his thorax. The game's greatest star turned the colour of putty.

My heart climbed into my throat. I raced out of my crease and brought my stick down upon Lacombe's helmet—I can still hear the sick cracking sound today—crumpling the rugged enforcer to

DAVE BIDINI

the ice. A swarm of Flames converged upon me, and Wayne's face bloomed. As I was being pulled to the ice, I shouted that I loved him.

The next thing I remember, the refs were leading Wayne and me off the ice. Television lamps flared from the rafters as "Achy Breaky Heart" wailed around the rink, the crowd screaming and beating the glass. The following day, newspapers ran a photo of us gliding into the camera lens— our sweaters torn and ravaged, shoulder straps hanging down, noses and mouths bloodied and broken, arms weak and defeated at our sides.

We looked fucking cool.

Our skates hit carpet. Under the runway canopy, we were escorted by two Alberta cops to our dressing room. The Gifted One spoke first:

"Fucking frog Lacombe. Goddamned piece of shit tried to kill me."

"Brutal," I said, staring up and down his body.

"I mean, fuck. He started in with the fag stuff, you know? Christ, I don't mind being called a fag, but not by some fucking pussy like him."

I stood up.

"Wassup, Squid? Don't worry. The guys'll pull 'er out."

"What happened out there," I told him, "I did it because I love you."

"What?"

"Shit. Fuckin' shit," I said, laying my fists against my head.

Wayne moved towards me. He looked into my eyes. He grabbed me around the neck, pulled his chest to mine, and sank his tongue into my mouth, reaching under my ass and hiking it into his groin.

He didn't really.

"Lissen, Squid, that's cool and everything, I mean I love you in a way too, man. But there's this girl, Janet. She's an actress."

Outside, I could hear the team roar down the hallway.

It sounded like they'd won.

Wayne ran to the door.

They'd be here any second.

JOAN

—One question: did you ever get jiggy with Joan?

—Who are you, MC Hammer?

—I was just trying to be polite.

—There's no room for polite in hockey.

—Ok. Did you ever bang her?

—Bang is too hard a word to associate with the ethereal loveforce that was Joan.

—Sorry.

—S'ok. And no. It hasn't come to pass.

—That's not what the guys think.

—They can think all they want.

—But you guys were close last year, weren't ya?

—Yeah. We made a connection.

—You stood up for her a lot. You took it all pretty personal.

—She was and is a beautifully talented goalie, her

eyes as bright as a dewy conifer wet with the dawn's first licking.

–Who said that? Wordsworth?

–No, I did. I put it in one of the poems that I never sent. I was going to give them to her before Fat Bob did you-know-what.

–We all thought you were gonna end up uglier than Jamie MacCoun once those bandages came off.

–Jamie MacCoun's not ugly. Tim Hunter is ugly.

–Hunter was only typically ugly. Jamie MacCoun was weird ugly. Troll ugly.

–Joe Thornton's like that.

–Yeah, but he pulls babes; he's a star. Being an ugly forward with good hands is one thing. Being a stay-at-home defenceman with a face like a pooch's arse is another.

–Well, it takes one to know one.

–Blow me.

–You brought it up. And as you can see, I retained my good looks despite Fat Bob's attempt to drive my nose through the back of my head.

–I thought that the stick-swinging era was long over, but you know, leave it to Fat Bob to beat a dead horse.

–Fucking psycho prickface.

–What was it you said, anyway?

–We were arguing about Joan. He was dead set against bringing a woman on board. I think he called her a fag right after he called me a dyke. He was getting that sort of stuff mixed up all the time.

–Fat Bob hated everyone.

–Friggin' macho dinosaur. Good thing I threw my jaw in the flight path of his Koho, eh?

–Helluva gesture, Ronnie.

–Truth is, I couldn't stand seeing him get in the way of Joan joining our team. The first time she left me the puck at the side of the net and said, "Have a good rush now," I thought I'd died and gone to heaven. No goalie had ever been so nice to me. Usually, it's all "You're fucking screening me! You're fucking screening me!!" But Joan's voice was as soft as a swallow's hum.

–Henry David Thoreau?

–Ben Harper. It just became very important for me to share the ice with her as much as possible. I thought it was important in terms of dragging our team out of the Stone Age, too, at least in a sporting sense.

–And you had the horn for her.

–She was beautiful! She is beautiful!

–Dude, that nose. I mean, it's not for everyone.

–A nose-bent-by-screaming-puck is very alluring, John. She's a female Patrick Roy with nipples like frosted cherries.

–That's weird.

–What's weird is that when trades happen in the NHL, I doubt that very many guys wonder what their new teammate is going to look like naked. I mean, I doubt that it's high on their list of questions.

–The wives ask those questions.

–You think?

–Oh yeah. I have a friend who dealt hash to the Kings in the '80s. When Billy Harris Jr. got sent there, my buddy was hanging out at Hammerstrom's place with the wives and the first thing they wanted to know was whether or not he had a big cock. They were excited that they'd have a new guy to fuck.

–Crazy.

–Crazy, true.

–Well, for me, Joan was as smart as she was beautiful and talented. A lethal combo.

–She was kinda weak on the short side, Bud.

–I can't stop thinking about her.

–You don't say. I never would have guessed.

–My first mistake was watching *The True Adventures of Mandy and Mercedes*, that hockey porno.

–Carmen Electra?

–Nah, more nondescript. You ever rent porn?

–Dude, I'm a twenty-first century male.

–For me, it's a terrible ordeal, renting porn.

–Why?

–Because nobody wants to be known as an onanist, John. Even though masturbation is something that draws the world together—music and language and a view of the celestial skies be damned—the act itself is not terribly dignifying. Whenever I rent porn, I'm worried that someone's gonna see me. I walk around like a fat man trapped in an air duct. My arms tick-tock at my sides, my legs clunk one in front of the other, my head sits like a heavy porcelain urn on my shoulders. I'm like a somnambulist drifting through a kind of horny fog.

–Ronnie, it's only porn.

–I know, but still. I have a few basic requirements for choosing the right place to rent porn. It can't just be anywhere. One of my rules is that the store can never be a solely erotic depot, with lurid neon on the outside. The place I go to is actually called Friendly Fruit and Cigarette. It's a proper establishment. If someone sees me going in there, they can't come to the obvious conclusion. There's only one thing a person can be doing in Super Adult Video, but Friendly Fruit and Cigarette presents a myriad of possibilities. I think the safest way to view, buy or rent pornography is to be thousands of miles from home, where nobody knows who the frig you are.

–I know a guy who once saw Ed Broadbent come

out of a sex shop in Soho. My friend did his patriotic duty and told him, "Dude, don't you realize? You're not safe anywhere!"

–You need major cover. I'm lucky because my video store also rents a smattering of legitimate films.

–How you can call the collected works of Rob Schneider legitimate is beyond me.

–Good point. But still, they're a great smokescreen to get to that white curtain at the back of the store.

–My place has saloon doors.

–Weird.

–Yeah. I think the pornkeeper thought it might add a touch of class.

–Friendly Fruit is pretty modest. The person who runs it is a sixty-year-old Asian woman. It's perfect because, in her eyes, every fumbling pervert represents another three dollars and forty-nine cents. She has an authoritative fortysomething son who sometimes works the counter. I hate it when he's there because he looks at me like I'm somehow the weaker of us, even though guys like me are keeping him in business.

–The only thing to do is become the shame, embrace it, celebrate it.

–Sometimes you have no choice. I rented *Mandy and Mercedes* at the Fruit and Smoke because the cover showed them sitting without pants in the dressing room. I carried the tape home like it was a bomb. I cradled it under my arm fearing that, at any moment, it might detonate and send Technicolor genitalia flying out of my Save On Books cloth bag. But it never did. The first scene took place in a dressing room. The only way you could tell that it was a hockey rink was from a pile of goalie equipment sitting in the corner. Mercedes—or was it Mandy?—picked up a pair of goalie gloves and went to work on the depanted Mandy—or was it Mercedes?—with the nub of her waffleboard, rubbing it lengthwise across her shorn land of promise. Dude, it was hot. The actresses' performances were unremarkable with the exception of the way they maintained their balance while writhing on the bench. Then I imagined that it was Joan lying there and I was done. It was all I could do not to suffer a season-ending injury. I eventually bought the tape.

–So that's when you asked her to join the team?

—Yeah, but it's not what you think. Not totally. I ran into her at the rink one afternoon. Dude, she has the most encyclopedic knowledge of hockey of anyone I've ever met.

—More than the Chizzler?

—Yeah, more than the Chizz. That's the thing: not only was she beautiful, but she was nerd-wild about hockey. The first time we drove anywhere together, I was rambling on about politics, trying to impress upon her that I had interests beyond the rink. You know what she did?

—What?

—She told me, "Quiet: I gotta hear this." It was the prime time sports round table and they were talking about whether Sauve or Kipper was gonna start in goal.

—Holy shit.

—I know. She was a dream. A friggin' impossible dream. Don't tell me you didn't catch any of that.

—No, I gotta admit that I did.

—You and Chizz. I've never seen you throw your bodies in front of pucks like that.

–Chizz asked her out. You knew that, right?

–No. I did not know that.

–I think he thought he'd found a kindred spirit.

–Anyone else?

–Anyone else what?

–Anyone else ask her out?

–Nah, most of us could see what she meant to you. We respected that. Some of the guys were into that other chick, her friend, what was her name?

–Sammi. I told you what happened, right?

–No.

–Joan told me that Sammi was coming to visit, and she asked if I wanted to come over for dinner and meet her and stuff. I said okay. By this time, me and Joan had become friends. We'd traded hockey books, watched games; she knew every player on every team, their tendencies, their history, all that. She knew way more than you about hockey.

–Again, I suggest that you blow me.

–Joan lived in a small townhouse. She lived alone.

I brought a bottle of wine and a compilation tape of Joan's best work that Murray's wife had shot from the stands, just in case Sammi was a hockey fan, which I figured she had to be. When I got there, Joan gave me a little tour of the place, then we sat down to eat. After dinner, the three of us drank a few bottles of wine, smoked some pot, had a hilarious time. We talked all night—about hockey, public education, Sammi's trip to Egypt, comic book art, rent control, and which player on our team had the biggest schwang.

–You told her the truth.

–Fuck, no. If I'd told her about Chizz, who knows what woulda happened.

–You're lucky, dude.

–Shit, I know. Anyway, after dinner we settled in the living room and I put in the highlight tape. Then I went to the washroom. While I was in there, I could hear a sound coming from the other room. It was the sound of two women moaning. Moaning and panting. No shit. I stepped back into the hallway; I couldn't believe my ears. The moaning got more heated and frenetic. I pressed my back against the wall, put my hand to my chest. One of the girls let out a scream, then Joan

said: "Uh, Ronnie. I think you better get in here."
I recoiled in horror, because it wasn't Sammi
and Joan who were moaning; it was Mandy and
Mercedes. *The tape.* I'd left the house in such a
state that I'd made the kind of bone-chilling faux
pas that will haunt me for the rest of my life:
mistakenly screening lesbian pornography for
the woman with whom I want to spend the rest
of my life.

–Holy fuck.

–I know. Sammi said to Joan: "Girl, that boob job
of yours is so the bomb." I lunged for the VCR.
Joan protested, but I couldn't even look at her.
I pulled the tape from the machine, stuffed it
into its box and put the box in a bag. Joan said:
"Ronnie, I never took you for a cinephile." Then
Sammi said she wanted to watch some more. I
didn't know what to do. I told them that I should
probably go, but Joan said that I definitely should
not. I was mortified, confused.

–Dude. How awful.

–Sammi lunged for the tape, but I stopped her.
Then Joan suggested that we roll another joint,
so we did. We smoked some more dope, got
wasted, and then Joan excused herself. Fifteen

minutes later, there was no sign of her, so me and Sammi went looking around. We found her passed out on the bed. It was around that time, I think, that Sammi reached down and grabbed my tool.

–A tool grabber!

–Yeah. Who knew? I was drunk, shamefaced; she was stoned and horny. She tore off my clothes and I responded in kind.

–You remember any of it?

–Not really. It was drunken panic sex.

–Which is still, technically, sex.

–Yeah, but drunken panic sex is pretty empty.

–Right, but again, technically . . .

–It's just that I'd always imagined sleeping with Joan, but instead, there was her best friend, trying to get me to lick her armpit.

–And?

–It was sort of minty. I cleaned up and got the frig home.

–Did Joan ever find out?

–What do you think?

–Of course she did.

–Sammi told her. I found out before game seven.

–Did Joan confront you?

–No, it wasn't like that. It actually wouldn't have come to light had you dickheads not suggested we change together.

–Well, it was a little like trying to get hamsters to mate, but everybody knew that you needed a little help in terms of sorting things out. Besides, she'd been changing all year by herself. We figured she needed a little company for such a big game.

–At first, I just sat across from her and said nothing. Then she started to undress. First, she took off her denim jacket and flannel shirt and kicked off her snow boots. She put them below the bench and buried her bracelet and necklace under the tongue. She unbuttoned the top of her jeans and tugged them over her hips, down her legs, then she lifted her T-shirt over her head. I couldn't believe what was happening. Her skin was bronze, her body knotted with muscle. Her arms and legs were as toned and lovely as spawning salmon.

–Leonard Cohen?

—No, Bill Murray. Anyhow, when she rose from the bench and took off her underpants, it was what I'd imagined millions of times in my head. My nerves were like a high-powered drill in the hands of a child, and I was shaking. Standing up, she tightened her fists, raised her hands above her head, and yawned. Her bush jumped like a cat playing with a mitten. And then I told her, flat out: "Joan, I had sex with Sammi." You know what she said?

—What?

—"I know."

—How did she know?

—That's what I asked her. But then she said: "Sammi told me later that night, right before we made love."

—Holy son of God.

—I said that I didn't know she was gay. Then she said that she wasn't gay. I should add that she was pulling on her jill at the time. A jill is like a jock only it's got this sexy curve up the side, not as blockish as a jock.

—An excellent detail.

–I told her that she was gay, and that Sammi was her lover. Then she said that Sammi was *my* lover.

–She had a point.

–I told her that she was gay and that I was a creep. And then I told her that I loved her.

–Oops.

–Then she conceded that she was bi. At this point she was dressed entirely in goalie gear. It was all very strange.

–Bi is good. Bi is, like, totally good!

–I told her that I never do anything I ever intend to do, and that I fumble around too long until the moment passes. I spilled my guts right there, John. And then she asked if that was my way of asking her out on a date.

–And you said it was, right?

–Yeah, I did.

–So?

–So she's coming over tonight.

–Excellent.

THE FIVE HOLE

–I'm nervous as hell. Really, dude, I love everything about her.

–You think you'll get jiggy with her?

–You're so 1989.

–If it happens, you know how you'll know it's forever?

–How?

–Right after you've done in your second bottle of wine and scraped the bottom of the bong and she's just finished waxing poetic about the career of Alan Bester, she reaches over and puts your hand right there.

–On her belt?

–No, not on her belt.

–Where then?

–On her five hole. You know, Ronnie, once you've found a goalie's five hole, they're yours forever.

I AM BOBBY WOLF

YOU ARE SPINNING
ROTATING
AN ORB

"MON DIEU!" they shout behind
the windows of their brasseries. "AY, MR. WOLF!
AY, MR. BOBBEEE!!" Fans clutter the sidewalks
waving napkins, placemats, postcards, coasters,
and magazines. One pudgy kid with a fat head
rushes out of his papa's butcher shop, handing
The Wolf a ballpoint pen and a white rag. "Papa
says he hate you," he spits. "But mama, she's in
love!" The Wolf signs it for the old woman, who'll
spread it across her night table under her prayer
candle, jewel box and tobacco tin filled with cotton swabs, moving her hand across the rough cloth
come playoff time while the old man lies prone in
his Habs red and blue, snoring and reeking of rot-
gut in the rumpled bed behind her. "My favourite
is Pierre Pilote!" says the boy, flashing narrow
eyes and chipped teeth, drool leaking from the
corners of his mouth. Within seconds, The Wolf

is horseshoed by people pressing closer, their faces rising to him, mouths agape. He looks away into the emptiness of the sky, where a kiss of pigeons flies out of an eavestrough, their milky brown bodies lost against a long cloud that drifts across the sky. Soon, the cops show up, flipping open their little yellow pads: "Geez, the boys down at the station don't know what they're missing!" TO MONTREAL'S FINEST: KEEP ON SHOOTING STRAIGHT. Taxis lean on horns and buses stutter and doubletake before the paparazzi arrive, snapping flashbulbs, shouldering him, trying to get under his coat. The Wolf holds up the flat of his hand—"That's all for today, folks!"—and steps into a waving taxi door, which closes onto an angry, tightening face that reaches out as they pull away, then pumps the big Go Fuck Yourself with his finger from the sidewalk.

IN SPACE IS PEACE
IN LIFE IS SPACE
BREATHE

"Your number one fan, eh?" asks the driver, a small man in a wool cap.

"One of them, I guess."

"Me, I'm a Beliveau man," he says.

"Helluva player," replies The Wolf, watching the crowd shrink.

"My boy admires your shot," he says, shaking his head. "That crazy shot."

"Thanks."

"I didn't say that I admired your shot," he says. "I think it's impure."

"Impure, eh?"

The driver laughs. "Back in the old days, it didn't take a blade that went this way and that way and this way to score goals," he says, making curving motions with his hand. "You played with a straight stick, something you pulled off a floorboard. A bed slat. Didn't need to do tricks. Players used to make that fucking puck sing with what they had."

"You don't like Boom Boom, either? He uses one."

"PAH! Boom Boom. He had one good year. My grandmère could score fifty with the chances he gets."

"I thought that every Hab was sacred around these parts."

"You think we French are blind to the nuances of the game, Bobby Wolf?"

"No, I didn't mean . . ."

"We drummed Donnie Marshall out of town, didn't we? Chewed up Mr. Worsely and spat him out like raw meat PLAH! We gave him three nervous breakdowns, you know," he says, waving his fingers in the rear view.

"Listen, I . . ."

"I've heard this kind of thing before. The English think the French are little blind dogs. Meep meep meep meep meep," he says, performing a talking pantomime with his hand. "I don't mean to judge, Mr. Bobby Wolf, but really. My passions lie not with a player simply because he wears the bleu, blanc et rouge. It helps, yes, but please, allow me this, okay?"

"Of course. I'm sorry."

"Don't be sorry, friend. Be worried. At this moment, the Habs' play is cresting. I don't have to remind you that you haven't scored in five games."

"Thanks."

"For what?"

"Not reminding me."

"You see, we French. We are clever, eh?" he says, stabbing his temple.

"Yes, very clever," sighs The Wolf, looking out

the window at the tree-lined street. Pappin's self-help tapes roll over in his mind: *The tranquility of the universe. The attitude of an empty sky. The simplicity of a woman's back.*

"What you need is a good salve," he says.

"I'm taking supplements."

"Pills," he scoffs. "Everything with a pill, eh? This salve is different. It's from the North. One dab on your scrotum and you'll be invigorated, Bobby Wolf. I am a simple taxi man, but this much I know: once you apply the salve, it is absorbed into the walls of the skin and then—sweeeeeeesh!—believe me, straight into the bloodstream!"

"If anything's gonna touch my ball sac, it better be attached to a woman."

"So proud, Bobby. But beware. Are you so proud that you think you can overcome the powers of this slump? Don't be foolish. This salve is magic."

"Thanks anyway."

"I know a man who takes it who is seventy-seven. Still, he fornicates!"

"That's swell."

"Carries twenty bushels of grain a day. Keeps a stable full of cows, goats."

"What's in it?"

"What?"

"The salve."

"Tree sap, cedar oil, man gel, beaver milk."

"Christ."

The driver swerves off St. Catherines and heads down a narrow alley.

"Quickly, we'll go."

"Where? No. I've got practice."

"It can wait. I am doing you a great favour, Mr. Bobby Wolf, star of the Hawks. You see? This Frenchman has a greater concern for the game!"

SEE THE SOUND
HEAR THE PICTURE
FEEL THE AIR

The house smells of old cushions. Emile puts The Wolf in a plastic-covered chair in the sitting room, and says, "Wait, Bobby Wolf," and hands him a pawed-over sports section from *La Presse*:

WOLF, QU'EST-CE QU'IL Y A?

The light is dim. The air dense, hot, thick. There's the sound of an old woman's voice through a door, then Emile rushing down a hallway. "Come with me," he says, returning to the sitting room. "My mother wants to see you."

The old woman is lying in bed. Above her is a huge wooden cross draped with beads and palms. Her eyes are barely open, but when The Wolf walks in, filling the door frame, she lifts her head and motions for him to approach.

He moves beside her and she grabs a handful of London Fog.

"Is it so bad that you must come to an old *vache* like me for help, Bobby Wolf?" she croaks.

"Mama," whispers the driver. "The salve."

"Your powers. Where are they now, Bobby Wolf?"

"It's only been two weeks," he tells her.

"Two weeks can be a lifetime, a career," she reminds him.

"Two weeks."

"Watch neither the calendar nor the clock, Bobby Wolf. Watch the stars. Time is passing through them. Time is being drawn across the skies. Do you remember Augustus Dupuis? He wore number twelve, I think."

"Mama, the salve."

"He was a star once. In my time, the twenties. Skated like the wind and possessed a shot like a rifle. Then one day, *saint siboire*, it was over. One game. Two. Five. Ten. Fifteen. Soon, he was holding his stick as if it were a gravedigger's tool, long and heavy, a burden to him. He was our favourite player. My parents sent me down to the rink to bring him birchbark tea, spiced meats, herbal tinctures. Of course, he refused to take any of it. A man once told me that Dupuis tried to drink his way out. Whored around the city, broken, desperate. Then: nothing. No goals in twenty games. We brought him the salve and he threw it into the street. I watched him. He had no respect for magic, the universe. And now, here you are standing in front of me. A star. You've never even heard of this man."

"I have now," he tells her.

"This is a start," she says, raising a single sepulchral finger.

The old woman reaches for her night table. She opens a drawer and hands him a vial filled with a gold liquid, then places her hand on The Wolf's.

"Rub this into your chestnuts," she says, coughing.

"What's in it?"

"Maybe your life," she says.

"That's an awfully small bottle for such an enormous thing," he tells her.

"You can laugh now, that is good. But laughter comes from the same place as sadness. A joke can be either tragic or funny, depending on the ending."

The old woman raises herself up on her elbows and pulls the London Fog closer to her face. Her breath is sour, her eyes half-alive.

"Your chestnuts," she croaks.

"My chestnuts," says The Wolf.

She closes her eyes.

PASS INTO THE VOID
PASS THROUGH THE VOID
FLOATING

Club Paris is the same every hour of the day or night: swirling lights, long couches, clacking beaded curtains, mirrored walls, the scent of desert root, coconut oil, lamb's breath. And, of course, women in every state of undress. Dancers from Grenada, Puerto Rico, Sept-Îles; men from Belgium, Toronto, The Hague. Bouncers wider than two-car garages with watering-can faces, all of whom immediately recognize The Wolf.

DAVE BIDINI

"Afternoon, Mr. Wolf," they say, "Greetings and salutations, Mr. Wolf."

He slivers the doorman a smile and palms him a twenty. He shows him to a private room, lit softly. In it, there's a settee, a glass table, a bucket with champagne on ice, and a bowl of fresh fruit. Music starts up outside: "Let me stand next to your FIRE!" As he leans forward and peers into the main room, a naked black chick in devil's horns is writhing on a small stage, dappling her body with globs of Day-Glo dripped from a paintbrush. The Wolf wonders if this is what Pappin meant when he said, "Temptation is the last step before the pain of self-discovery." But before he can know, there's a taste in the air.

Her hair is sandy, her skin golden. Sylvie looks at him and says, "My boy is having trouble filling the net, yes?"

"I've been listening to these tapes," he tells her.

"And what do these tapes say?" she asks.

"They tell me to keep myself open to the forces of the universe."

"Come with me," she says, taking his hand. "I know how to find these forces."

Sylvie takes him to a room painted hot orange.

They lie on a round bed, with orange posts and an orange headboard. There's a record player in the corner shaped like a space pod. With long black fingernails, she flips up the top, moving the tone arm to a Marvin Gaye album that begins with a wah-wah guitar and ends, a half-hour later, with the heartbeat of a single bass drum.

"It's been five games," he says, lying naked across the bed.

"And your team is losing?" she asks, playing with the hair on his arm.

"No, no. Mikita's scoring."

"Well, then, perhaps if the universe is not open to you, it is open to him."

"Stan doesn't have those concerns. He's Czech. He worries about what the next day's going to bring. Coming from abject poverty will do that to you."

"Your family was not poor?"

"We grew up on a farm. I guess we were poor. I never felt poor."

"How do you feel now?"

"Not poor."

"Well, then."

"Sylvie, I've been given this salve."

"Salve?"

"A lotion. An old Québécoise woman told me it would restore my powers."

"How old was this woman?"

"Old as dirt."

"It is best not to ignore the practices of old French women. They have survived for many years living by the same means."

"Her son brought me to her in his taxi. Funny little guy."

"What did she say to do with this salve?"

"She told me to coat my chestnuts."

"Your chestnuts?"

"You know," he says, pointing between his legs. "Chestnuts."

"Oh," says Sylvie, covering her mouth and giggling. "Well, then. Where is it?" she asks, reaching for his coat.

"There's no need to . . ."

"This streak is in your chestnuts?" she asks, getting up.

"Pappin says it's a problem with my chi, my spiritual equilibrium," says The Wolf, watching Sylvie rise off the bed to stand naked in front of him, spreading the golden salve into the palm of her hand.

"I like a man who is concerned about his

spirit," she says, stretching out beside The Wolf, her face lying flat against his stomach.

"No goals in five," incants The Wolf.

"The goals will come. You are Bobby Wolf."

"Maybe the answer to my problem is right here in front of me," he tells her, watching her position her shoulders between his legs. "Maybe it's right here and I don't even know it."

"I am a French woman. One day I will be an old French woman," she says, working her arm with the strength and elegance of a swan's neck. "Yes. I am a French woman," she repeats, "and you are Bobby Wolf."

The salve is warm on his skin.

"You are Bobby Wolf."

Bobby Wolf closes his eyes and dreams of pigeons returning to the trough.

"How does that feel?" she wants to know.

Suddenly, he is light, free.

RIDE WITH THE AIR
YOU CAN
YOU WILL

"You are Bobby Wolf," whispers Sylvie.

"I am Bobby Wolf."

DAVE BIDINI

CORTINA

Stephen Jackson (RW) was a hard-nosed career minor-leaguer from Odie, Saskatchewan (pop. 410) who played for seventeen seasons. He toiled largely in the ECHL, AHL, USHL, and CHL, and attended various NHL training camps, but was inevitably among its final few cuts. His rambunctious play, heavy shot and noted junior career (Saskatoon Blades) promised a greater pro legacy than was delivered. Still, that he was able to stay in the game for so long supports his perseverance—and stubbornness—as an athlete.

June 22

Cousin Joanie told me to get this writing book because she thot I shude try to remember everything that happened to me because, she sed, the only people from Odie who'd ever gone to Europe had gone during the last war, and even then, lots of men went, but few came home. And those who wrote back mostly wrote about how much they missed home, even tho there isn't much to miss, not in

Odie, not hardly. So I did like Joanie sed and got a book and a pen at the airport in Newark, and I'll tell you, old page, I feel like someone else sitting here at this donut table scribbling out what for me is more words than I've written since Ms. Cartwright told me to print I WILL NOT THROW INK IN THE FISHTANK 30 tymes on the blackboard in Grade 6 class after, ya, I threw ink in the fishtank. In our classroom. Some weerd white-ish specks came over the fishes and they got all plumpy. And then they died, and, ya, I felt bad for at least a year, maybe more, even tho hockey fans might not think that players cry or feel bad, but they do, probably even worse than most. What was I saying?

Stephen Jackson's best season came in 1999/2000 while playing for the Omaha River Ducks of the Central Hockey League. He scored twenty-five goals and thirty-three assists, finishing tenth in league scoring. He was largely the benefactor of teammate Stan Crashley's (C/LW) breakout year. In 1999/2000, Crashley scored fifty goals for only the second time in his career and was awarded the Harold Lawrence Trophy for MIP (Most Improved Player). Crashley and Jackson would play three more years together at various minor hockey outposts, eventually ending their careers with Cortina of the IHL (Italian Hockey League).

April 7

Crashley is my buddy from Omaha (River Ducks) and Providence (The Reds). He's the one who told *me about Itly. I sed the name of the place back to him, but he sed, There's a sound in there between the t and the l, even tho it was news to me. I'd always sed: Itly. But there was a sound in the middle, which was good to know seeing as I'd be playing there. For Cortina. Parmalat. Whatever that means.*

Sometymes, life is weerd. Not that I'm complaining. I've seen far worse in Odie, especially with the young ones now, and how they get into tattooing their faces and sniffing gloo and huffing gas before hiking down to The Toon, where they dry up like old corn husks once they start with the meth. Hockey saved me from all that, and it contin-yous to save me, old page (as you're well aware). What was I saying? I remember: Itly. As a hockey player, you have no tyme for nothing, let alone learning the names of countries you never think you'll visit, and, in some cases, don't want to visit. Mom and Dad went to Itly wonce, before they moved to Odie. I saw the pictures: dad in his shorts, dark socks and sunglasses, mom all beehived and cool smoking a cigarette in a sleeveless blouse. "Tooring Europe" is what they called it, as if they wer the Chris de Berg band or something. Still, because they'd gone there, I felt like part of me had gone there too. Is that weerd?

June 5

Arnie Roomes is the couch of the Parmalats—that can't be their name, can it? Doesn't sound too scary, unless of course it's some kind of strange Italian animal I've never seen before (note to old page: beware of parmalats). The first tyme I talked to Roomes, it was from a pay phone in an old arena somewhere in Pennsylvania. He sounded like a man fed up with the sound of his own voice. I wrote down what Arnie sed:

You'll get a nice place in the city and they'll pay for a car. I can give ya thirty minutes a game if ya want it. Ya want it?

I told him that I did.

Then I asked where Cortina was compared to the rest of Itly.

Him: How the Hell do I know? I can tell you

where the rink is, tho, or at least how far it is from
the chicken ranch.

Crashley sez that Arnie wears a fedora and
never takes off his trenchcoat. He is what hockey
players call a souse or a pisstank—I don't mind
using this kind of language, seeing as writing is
private and everything—or an alkee. You might ask
How can he couch a hockey team and kill twenty-
seven Buds a day? but in sports, this is nothing.
I am NOT a pisstank, but I tell ya killing a case
on the weekend or drinking a dozen cans after a
SWEET victory is what you do. You learn it from
a young age. The asistant couch in my 1st year in
junior—Pidge was his name—was always giving
us booze when we had a good game or two. He'd
bring it up to our rooms and even drink it with us,
sometymes til late, late, late at night. In hockey, this
can be either good or bad news, because it depends
on who your couch is. A bad couch uses booze for
other things. I don't know how personal to get in
this storee, old page, but there are sickos out there
who shude be cut down at the first sign they are
using booze for anything other than a typical good
tyme. I know some players who drank with their
couches who will never get to Itly, if they ever get
to anywhere at all.

DAVE BIDINI

Arnie, I am talking about Arnie. So, he is a pisstank, but he can couch. Not that I know this first hand, but I tell ya I've herd it from Crashley, which is good enough. I trust Crashley, the fuckhead (you might think I am cursing him, old page, but I mean good fuckhead, not bad fuckhead). Crashley's blonde hair swoops up like a wave of lemon merang, and he likes to ware a leather coat with a fur collar (Skeez wonce sed he looked like a tranny hooker, which made me laugh my guts out). Crashley also likes outrayjous clothes and platform shoes, and is a prakital joker, which is one way to tell if a guy is a good guy or not. The year I roomed with him in Saltana—which was the worst; by which I mean, the best—he did things like change the clock radio so that I'd wake up and think that I missed practice. He put salt in my waterglass and a snake in the team towel basket. Wonce, he set the couches' shoes on fire, but only because Couch Trammel was named Couch of the Year (otherwise, he woulda got cut). Anyhow, when Crash tells you stuff, you beleeve it. And no, Itly isn't a joke, even tho I've got this tickle at the back of my head, which is also the feeling I get just before I get a cold.

THE FIVE HOLE

Stephen Jackson's career is typical of many aspiring pros whose hockey lives get caught in the game's spokes. For almost twenty years, Jackson lingered in the body of hockey, in its veins, bones and serrated teeth. He'd spent years in junior B mining towns, Maritime shanties and Canadian winteropoli—Regina, Winnipeg, Quebec. He'd played for teams named after animals he'd never heard of or seen: the Jackalopes, the Roadrunners, the Stags. He'd been an Ice Baron, an Ice Pirate—known, famously, around the league as "Ass Pirates"—an Ice Owl and, near the end, an Ice Monster in Lowell, where Jackson was once wrongly suspended for a record twenty games after being attacked in the penalty box by a three-hundred-pound exotic dancer named Morganna, who came at him with a shoe (a stiletto; Jackson was never the type of player lucky enough to find himself on the hurtful end of a loafer). One of his former coaches, James Brody of the Columbus FireBlades, told the *Ohio Packet and Times* that, "Jackson tended to let the game slug him as much as it wanted, so long as he got his shifts."

Stephen played on Dollar-Beer Night, Four-for-One Corn Dog Night, Clown Wrestling Night, and Party 'Til You Pee Night, where three contestants were required to sit at a little table at centre ice drinking beer during the second intermission, and the last to urinate won a month of free lanes at the Tempe Bowlerama. After being traded to Skookum of the WCHL in 2003, Jackson told writer William Gaston that he'd "worn every kind of sweater: purple, teal, mauve, grey-brown, raspberry, and seventeen different shades of red. I've skated with more guys from countries ending with (the suffix) '-istan' than anybody should have to remember, guys whose last names practically slid off their shoulder down their sleeve. I've spat teeth and cracked bones and pulled ligaments in seventeen states and eight provinces over this humfrickin' planet of ice, which I discovered the first time I lifted my eyes long enough from my train set to see Glenn Anderson swoop like a heron through four defenders and flick the puck into the net like a guy tossing a coin off the end of his thumb. I was hooked, you know, and that was that."

In his book, *Deep Sea Hockey Stories*, Gaston wrote that: "Jackson was, famously, never the quickest cricket in the grass. He moved over the earth with great deliberation—a large, square man with soft, heavy-lidded eyes and the tendency to sigh before speaking or leaving a room. Even when he grew angry, his expression rarely changed, but for a quick hardening of the upper lip. He carried himself through life like a great toy whose batteries were forever low. Following him around on the day of our interview, I noticed that he protracted handfuls of minutes doing even the simplest things, like choosing what tin of soup to take off the shelves at the Maxi-Mart on Elm, which is where he shopped for all of his groceries and supplies. Jackson was the kind of person who gave the impression of mild discomfort when squeezing a sentence out of his head—a sentence which usually ended with one of two words— 'outstanding' or 'awesome'—perfectly good words, if less outstanding and awesome when repeated seventy times a day. Once, after he was asked by a teammate what the shrimp and scallop combo at the Red Lobster off I-50 near Marysville was like, you could see Jackson think hard and for a long time before he hoisted his thumb and announced: 'I'd have to say that it was outstanding.' When the teenage clerk in the red-striped frock handed him change for his Mexicali sub in the taco shop at the strip mall across from where he lived, I heard him tell her, 'Just so you know, ma'am, the seasoning on the Mexicali was awesome,' before wishing her an outstanding day. I think that Jackson sensed that if he spent just a little longer searching for a different adjective, he might have stopped at 'magnificent' or 'wondrous' or 'breathtaking,' words that clearly flitted across his consciousness before ducking into the recess of his brain. Because he'd spent so many evenings getting hit with the puck in dark rinks, his voice had also slurved the way a song slows when you press your thumb on the record. Jackson gave the impression that he'd never seen the bottom of Grade Six, but in fact, I learned that he'd aced high school math and graduated sixtieth in his class out of one hundred and eighty. Which isn't Albert Einstein, but it's not Ralph Wiggum, either."

June 4

The plane is going above the clouds. I'm pretending that I'm in a Van Damme movie and we are flying to a place called Omsk or Kartoom or Doobeye. I think the stewardess likes me. She's tall with legs up to here and nice firm roundish tits packed tight into her nice white blowse whose buttons I want to munch into dust with my teeth. Why do I get horny on planes, old page? Maybe it was the story Crash told me about the mile high club. I dunno.

Still: you never really know when you're going to get prowled. Wonce, back when I used to get my whiteouts, I passed out on the floor of a jewlery store (why I was in a jewelry store I don't know). When I woke up, the clerk—she was waring a purple pantsuit with her hair tied in a big tangle-nest high above her hed—asked if I played for the Ice (not Ass) Pirates, and when I sed that yes I did, she got out an ottograf pad and leaned over me, resting her elbow on my cock. It was nice, sure, but there was the sort of pressing issue of trying to see if I might ever stand up again. I went bak a few weeks later, old page, and she blew me in the dressing chambers. Don't worry, I wasn't with anyone at the tyme. But here, in the silence of all of this scribbling, what would it really matter?

June 9

I guess I have to tell you about the whiteouts. And the headaches. They wer very bad for a long tyme, but doc gave me some blue pills that I think (I hope) are going to work. He gave me 100, and told me what to eat in Itly cuz he's been there, like, 40 tymes (I forget what he told me. Weerd things). He sed that what happens to me—why I sometymes get spagetti legs on the ice without

any warning (Spagetti with clams, he sed. I
remember now), why I see the Curious Man with
Two Heads, why birds okassionally frighten me,
why the television news anchorman sometymes
sounds like he's eating steak instead of speaking
English, why 31s look like 26s, or why I wonce
missed training camp in Minot and ended up in
Wyoming, lost and trying to remember my name.
He sed that all of this happens to me because of
the tyme Robbie Ray pounded me one weekend
night in Plattsberg. Our fight was going good, at
least for me. I was getting in a few uppercuts. But
then BLAAMMO! he hit me below the eye. It was
like a balloon popping in my head. The roof of my
mouth started poring blood and I got all crosseyed
and blurry. So I covered and jabbed, covered and
jabbed. All I was thinking, was: don't hit me
there, not there, not again. I covered and jabbed,
covered and jabbed (where wer the zebras?) but
then BLAAMMO! he hit me in the same place.
And then the walls came tumbling down. Someone
sed that I think. In a song. Wait, here comes the
tightee waitress.

Jackson was among the most injured players of
his time. While lower minor league injury reports

aren't as reliable as the AHL or NHL's, it can be established from local newspaper reports that Jackson spent more stretcher time than any other player in history while also suffering the fewest loss of minutes. There are only three occasions, from what this writer can tell, where he had extended stays on the DL—Pimberton (1998, twenty-three games: fractured skull); Plattsburg (2001, thirty-one games: broken orbital, cheekbones, lacerations of the face); and Red River (1996, fifteen games: concussion)—which is remarkable considering that he played in North American hockey's toughest and most violent leagues.

June 17
Did I mention this already? When I asked Arnie where he wanted my agent to send my medical records—or not send them, seeing as he'd stopped talking to me after my third demotion—he sneezed into his hand and sed

You got a dick and two feet, don't ya?

I wanted to tell him, Well sir, I do most tymes, but did not. Anyhow, I made the team (Just thot you shude know).

July 8

It's like a gingerbread town, this place, this Cortina.
It's like what Jully the Baker used to put in his shop
window at Christmastime: little moustache men in
hats, women in long coats, crumloads of pidgeons,
and the smell of chocolate and pastrees in the air.
I probably don't have to point out the obviosity
of this, but: Cortina hockey is pretty difrent from
what I'm used to. I'm used to riding around on
buses sitting next to wannabe Gretzkys bitching
about how their hack couch grinding out some
personal vendetta is standing in their way of glory.
I'm used to Pizza Hut and Spectravision, burnt
lobby coffee and Boston balls for lunch money,
and hours waiting for my agent to call to say he'd
found me icetyme in San Jose or Nashville—a call
that never came, old page. In the minors, me and
the boys read the stat pages of the Hockey News
the way old women read obitch-you-aries, looking
for death in the minus 40 players, thinking: Man,
that shude be me, not Boggy, sucking crud in the
bigs. What was I saying?

I remember. In ItAly the bus stops for three
hours at beautiful mountinside resorts, where we
eat 40 course lunches with wines that sell in corner
stores for the price of a pack of breath mints. One

more tyme, old page: we drink WINE at lunch.
No wonder the old pisspot loves it here. The
rink is like a winter fantasy. There are windows
around the building that fill the arena with natural
light. Everything is fresh and beautiful, even the
popcorny upper parts of the stands. Outside the
building there's a valley, where little twists of
chimney smoke come up from the shalays below.
Our team is called the Jets. I'm a Wop Ducky
Hawerchuk, and yes, I do like it.

In 2005, Jackson was recruited by the Cortina
Parmalat Jets of the IHL, perenially the league's
basement dwellers and coached by defrocked
NHL coach Arnie Roomes. Roomes brought over
a handful of Canadian and American pros to
improve his team's fortunes. At first, this experi-
ment proved unsuccessful, but with the addition
of Stan Crashley, the Jets earned a first division
league promotion, and later, with Jackson and
others, they competed for the A League (Serie A)
title. In '05, Roomes, who has since been heralded
as a European innovator for his introduction of the
Italian game to North American hockey culture,
told Mark Akbab of the *Hockey News*: "Truth is,
I brought in guys from back home because I was

sick and tired of trying to learn Italian. I decided to get some Canadian-speaking players so that I didn't go friggin' nuts."

July 28

I've met a chick, old page. Her name is Franchessca. She is a dark lampost of a girl with long shiny black hair and cheekbones that make me think of a painting of Pokeahontas I used to keep hidden under my bed, and used for certain untoward purposes. Fran is like a bubbling fountain, a firework going off. Her hands are always moving. At first, I thot we wer gonna ploink right there in the AMERICAN IDOL disco because of the way she touched me when we talked—gripping a shoulder, tapping a breast bone, squeezing an arm—but then I learnd that this is how pretty much every Italian behaves. Coming from Odie, where you can't sit next to a girl in the backseat of the car unless you're married, it was great. But at the end of the night, you know what she did? She pressed her palm to her lips, then pressed it against my cheek. I wrote down what she sed (I mean, Johncarlo wrote it down for me):

Ciao, bellissimo. Vediamo, eh, amore?

Four out of those five words, I don't understand.

*I asked Crashley what he thot she meant (stupid
idea, ya, I know). This is what he sed:*

*I think she was telling you to put your trouser
snake back in its cage.*

Me: That's what I was afraid of.

*Him: Whatever you do, don't be afraid, Hoss.
As soon as a chick smells fear in a guy, she'll rip
your lungs out.*

Me: But she'd be worth it, dontcha think?

*Him: Dude, why settle for a head case when
there's an army of Wop pussy out there waiting to
jump your bones?*

Aug 8

*Fran and I hang out along The Garden Wall. The
Garden Wall is "the city's weedy, thousand year
old partition which seperates Cortina from the
Alpine valley running north to Bavaria" (it sez
this in the pamflet that I found in my apartment).
It's where young ones in heat neck and play hide
the salami. It's alot like my old junior hockey days
when I used to dry-hump fether-haired highschool
chicks named Jada and Jasper in their torned-up
denim jeans behind the portables. Camel toes.
Wheelchair Chemo Skunk Weed. AC/DC. Sweet
cheeks packed like basketballs into hot sexy gym*

shorts. There was lots of skank in the minors, too, skank that wouldn't have known what to do with a Garden Wall (maybe stradle it, I dunno). But Franchesssca IS NOT skank. Skank is something that might get stuck to the sole of her shoe. I know this because I tried a few skank moves on her, but she slapped my hand and sed BASTA! (this means STOP!) right before she pushed her tongue into my mouth, which I sucked like warm toffee. Then she turned and headed home, her hips going this way and that like the ticktocking of a clock (a friggin sexy clock). Back in my apartment, I peeled my dick from the inside of my pants, then played out the rest of the evening in the cold light of the bathroom.

When I interviewed Crashley for this piece, the former Harold Lawrence Trophy winner told me that "Jax fell in love with a woman in Italy. I mean, we all fell for the women over there, but Jax was really taken with her, you know. After a while, it was pretty hard to get him to come out with us, which was strange because Jax was the most team-oriented guy I'd ever met." It's been stated by lots of hockey experts that one of the reasons for the recent flood of players to Italy is the social culture of some of Europe's most swinging cities. For the aging player who's spent their career wandering contract to contract through low US cities with barely a passing interest in the game, Italy can be a trove of experience. That said, I asked Crashley what he thought about Italy's deeply conservative approach to sexuality among young people. In this writer's experience, I've found an aura of sexual repression in what many perceive, incorrectly, as the most open society in the world. Italians, traditionally, have been bound by the wrath of the church, the scorn of *la mama*, and the conservative nature of a three-thousand-year-old society unchanged since medieval times. All of this is set, impossibly, against a parade of naked women cavorting in detergent ads and talk shows on Italian television; bus shelters, billboards and magazine covers bounding with naked body parts; and an almost theatrical sense of sexuality that pervades the singles' set, which exudes caged lust against a culture of intoxicating wine, food and art. I proposed my theory to Crashley. I asked if the ironies of ItaloCulture proved difficult to stickhandle around. He told me:

"Uh, no."

At practice, Crashley, Skeez, and Lurch brag about how many tymes they've sunk their pole (and lookat me, I'm an o'fer). All of that is fine, but you've got to watch out for Skeez, cause it was bad behayvyour that put him here, even tho he's got talent to burn. Skeez is what I'd call a Walking Hard On. He's into bar fights, coke/crack and Dick Tricks, meaning that he likes to pose with it tied in a knot (the Pretzel) or stuffed between his legs (the Madonna). Skeez is also really tuff on rookies. He made two Swedish rooks gaffer tape his dick to his leg (he told them that it got in the way of him skating right). Then he made them crawlrace on the dressing room floor with a kookie up their arse, and the loser had to eat the kookie. This is Skeezer's thing, this is his fun. He was run out of Dallas in the NHL because he got the VP's daughter pregnant, but then she tried to off herself, and that was a terrible thing. I don't know if this means anything but Skeez was raised pretty ruff in a bad part of Winnipeg and his mom was a whore, if the kind of whore who drove him to practice and bought him skates in between backalley suckjobs. So when Crashley told me about this party down in the valley, my first question was whether Skeez was going, a question that I knew the answer to before I'd even asked it. Still, Fran is heading to Treest (her uncle is sick) and the blueballing is driving me crazy.

Sept 5

Tonight was dinner at Fran's. It was her send off to Treest. Everyone was shouting and eating and it was very noisy and fun. We ate outside under a seeling of grapes. Fran's place is as loud as Chicago Stadium, which is weerd because in Odie, it's usually so quiet you can hear the next door neighbor's chair scraping back. Fran's granny is an old shrivelled lady who wears black and when she met me she started crying and couldn't stop. And then Fran's mom started crying, then her aunt, and then Fran, too, and they didn't stop until the old lady let go of my hand, which she squeezed tight as a vice. I stood up and felt pretty dizzy and was actually worried that the whiteouts wer coming back, but it was just everything about the seen, and probably, all of the strange misteryous crying. I took Fran in my arms and she hugged me tight. Then we went out to the street, and here's what she sed (I wrote it down):

After the season is over, we will learn more

about each other. You will be with my family, be part of us. It will be as it shude be.

Me: That would be outstanding.

Her: You say 'outstanding' so much. Is this the poetry of Canada?

Me: 'Poetry' makes it sound too good, I think.

Her: Perhaps you wer a poet—perhaps a painter—in another life. Maybe before the beginning of your hockey game.

Me: Don't think I haven't painted before. I've done my Uncle Jenk's place three tymes over. You keep painting the barn but the wind rips it off again.

Her: I'd like to see this one day.

Me: Oh, you say that. And don't think that it wouldn't be outstanding if I brought you back to Odie. But it's a big deal if someone from town wins the triple at Bingo. It's all over the papers the next day.

Her: We are together, I don't mind.

Me: I'm sure your family would love to see you move to Odie.

Her: Perhaps they will move too.

Me: And perhaps Arnie Roomes will find Jesus Christ. But I doubt it.

Things started to go awry for Jackson, it appears, around the latter half of the Jets' season, and through the playoffs. He was hit by the injury bug, once again, and missed various games despite being on track to set personal bests in goals and assists (and PIM, too). In a league with very little fighting, Jackson was undoubtedly the heavyweight champion. Reasons given for his demise have been wild and varied. Former Columbus Blue Jacket and Dallas Star John Skeeton—whom this writer tried to contact during his time in Renfrew Detention Centre (I was denied access, but a few letters were exchanged)—wrote to me, cryptically: "We all had the clap. We all got the slap. We shwapped and shwapped 'til it all went splat." There's no denying that this is a reference to a sexually transmitted disease, but whether this led to the end of Jackson's career is uncertain.

Aug 5

My dick hurts, old page. The cause of this was an orgy. Yes. I AM NOT KIDDING.

An orgy.

We got there in Crashley's little car after 20 miles of steep mountin road. There wer torches along the driveway then a big wooden door. A weerd skullish guy in a servant's vest took our coats in what I beleev people call a vestibule, and pointed to a big giant banquet hall where some classical music was playing. It was full of deep-eyed hotties in tight dresses, and hard-chested men in turtlenecks who looked like ski-ers, maybe French, maybe German, maybe both. Further down a long hallway was another room, then another after that, and then after that, THE ROOM—fluffy rugs and a mountin of pillows and candles shining across a field of booty and weeners. Skeez, of course, was the first to dive in. Me, I got both uptight and loose at the same tyme, but before I could decide which it was gonna be, a chick with peerced boobies wearing a cat eye mask pushed me under a scaffold of legs, arms, torsos, sacks and tits. My heart leapd like a mouse, but everything took care of itself. Suddenly, big Xmas tart nipples wer coming at me and people's fingers and toes were running over my body like loosed spiders. There wasn't a moment when Little Stevie wasn't being licked or tugged or pumped. Wonce, I saw Crashley, lying flat on his back a few feet to my right. I gave him the thumbs up, right before two chicks climbed aboard and ground theirselves on the old tranny's mug.

THE FIVE HOLE

There wer some very old people in the orgy.
This freaked me out, even tho it was interesting
in a syintific sort of way, seeing all of that
blotched pink and stretched boobs and crooked
finger weenees. Still, being an athlete helped in
this circumstanse cause I was able to pinch and
roll whenever one of them came in for me, their
sweaty wrinkled hands and drooling lips reaching
for Little Stevie like a fat boy to a lemon twizzler.
Skeez put on a show. He hauled chicks over his
shoulder, threw them down, screwed them. He
hollered YARRRGGHLLL and beat his chest, his
dick bouncing up and down. His eyes wer like little
hot stars, he was out there, stoned on sex. Worse,
I saw him do what I thot was fight with another
naked dude, only it turned out he wasn't fighting.
Seeing as writing is private and everything, I can
tell you, old page, that he was actually fucking
with the dude, and while it was hard to know for
sure, I'm pretty sure he was getting done by the
dude's rod, and not the other way around. On the
ride home, nobody sed nothing. Not a word. But I
am a real bad fuckhead, old page, because the next
morning the only person I could think of was

her.

DAVE   BIDINI

William Gaston, the novelist, had mentioned to me while I was researching this piece that there existed, in one form or another, a diary that Jackson had kept while playing in Italy. Serious efforts were made to try to find these pages, but every lead turned out to be a blind alley (Jackson's parents refused any kind of correspondence). Then I learned through Stan Crashley that Jackson had a cousin, Joan Jackson, with whom he was close. I flew cross-country the next day in an attempt to contact her.

Sept 6

I don't know what's going on old page things just get more confusing every day not just hockeywise but sexwise and Franwise. What happened was we wer at my place one afternoon when all of a sudden Fran drew the drapes and took off all of her clothes except for her panties. Then she stripped me down except for my jeans and found my mouth and worked it with hers kissing and necking for what seemed like a long time right there in the semi-darkness of my apartment. It was all slow and great and on purpose, which was, of course, totally diferent from my crazy mountin orgyfuck, the events of which came to a hed after

THE FIVE HOLE

Crashley acted out some fagstuff in the dressing room around Skeez and then Skeez freeked out and started screaming and swung at him and broke two bones in his hand. Bad bad shit, old page. Bad. What was I saying? Oh ya: when I opened my eyes I could see Fran's small breasts and dark coastline body and stomach twisting with the moment. We moved across each others bodies like blind people dwelling on a peninsoola a fissure a mound of skin frozen by the power and beauty of the moment but then I got on top of her and she said, no.

Basta.

She pulled her knees to her stomach.

What? Let me, here . . .

I cannot do this terrible thing.

It's not terrible. It's not terrible.

Not terrible, no. Beautiful.

She put her face on her knees.

Powerful. I mean, powerful.

She made a small fist with her hand.

Oh, Fran. Shit.

My dick jumped, then fell.

I have made a promise to my family, to God.

You've seen me now. I hope this is enough for you.

DAVE BIDINI

No, shit. I'm dying here.
Dying?
No, not dying.
No.
I'm sorry, bello.
Oh, baby.
I am sorry.
Oh, baby. Shit. Shit.
Shitfuck.

Joan Jackson lives alone in a one-room apartment above her father's barber shop in downtown Odie, which isn't really a downtown, at all; rather, it's a single, boardwalked street with two stoplights. There are three points of convergence in Odie: the post office, the bar, and the hockey rink. Odie lost its church to a fire five years ago and they've yet to raise the funds to build another.

I tried to speak with Joan, but my appeals fell on deaf ears. Whenever I frequented the Jacksons's barbershop, I was stonewalled by the townsfolk and by Mr. Jackson himself. After it became clear that I would be staying in Odie for longer than a few days — well, not in Odie, but in a small motel located in nearby Frog Lake — he simply closed the shop. I'm fairly certain that Joan stayed in her apartment and never left. One morning, I awoke to discover that a shovel had been rammed through my car's windshield.

I left a note under the door of the barbershop and moved on to other research. Attempts to obtain medical records from the Jets proved even more fruitless than trying to obtain them from the North American minors. Worse, the Jets had folded before my research had started, and almost all traces of the team had vanished. Arnie Roomes died this past year of a heart attack. He, himself, leaves a very muddy hockey legacy.

But a few weeks before this collection of minor league profiles was to be submitted for publication, an envelope arrived in the mail containing ten pages of scribbled-over foolscap paper folded inside. What I found in that envelope is reprinted here. It answers a few questions about the final episode in the life of Stephen Jackson, but it leaves just as many unanswered.

Oct 7
The headaches are like fists pounding on an iron gate. At first, I thot this was because of those long weekdaynightsdrinkinganddoingcokeattheIDOL, but then I couldn't sleep, and then I couldn't skate

hard, and now alls I'm waiting for is the Curious Man With Two Heads to come around or the radio to start sounding like nonsensejumblespeak again. I got a new prescription after my 100 finished but they don't work, old page. The team doctor sez that they're the same but I don't see how this could be and besides the timing is terrible because we just started the playoffs against San Remo and last night I played like a halfman/halfgoat. I had no zip to my shot, no push to my legs. Resting on the bench was like no rest at all. At tymes, my vision got narrow and dark, like a person fiddling with a light socket. I stayed in the dressing room for the beginning of third period, then Arnie came in and yelled all kinds of stuff at me.

You've been hitting those shittin' sex parties, haven't you?

You know about them?

Know about them? One tyme, I caught something that nearly made my dick fall off. The worst dose I ever got. You seen the doctor about it?

About what?

About whatever it is that's got you skating like some crippled piece of shit Bambi out there.

I know, couch. Sorry.

Anyone else with ya?

Where?

Up the hill. You know.

I can't tell you.

The Hell you can't. I've got friends all over town. Well, not friends. But I'm gonna hear it eventually. Better just tell me now.

Crash, Skeez, Lurch. Crash brought us.

Four of ya? Christ.

Don't tell them.

Jesus Fucking Christballs.

I love those guys, Arnie. Don't tell them.

Those guys aren't all that you love, Slick.

Sept 7

The doctor did some tests then he phoned and asked if I had a girlfriend. I sed that I did. Then he sed:

Va Benne (this means GOOD). Come and see me. Bring her.

Sept 10

We lost to San Remo and the season is over but we played great in the deciding game. Lurch tied it on a shot from the point with 30 seconds left and the rink exploded with noise and even in my hazy fuzzy state I could see that it was a beautiful moment. Then they won it at the beginning of OT and in the dressing room afterwards Skeez was a mess a reck a river of tears balling his eyes out in the room saying how sorry he was to everyone before he started crying so hard you couldn't understand

a humfrickin' word of what he was saying. We tried to cheer him up but it didn't help at all. He just sat there bent over at the stomach waling for like twenty minutes until I went over and put my arm around him and pulled him to my shoulder and patted his head and even then the team doctor had to give him a needle to calm him down.

Sept 6

We were there in the little doctor's office, old page, and it was ok. Clean mountain light was coming in across the room through a big giant window. It warmed the arms of my chair, and made the fine wood of the doctor's desk look golden and I dunno kind of heavenly, I guess. Fran was sitting beside me. I was waring my blue Parmalat track suit and Addidas. The doctor brought out some papers. He folded his hands and sed:

Your X Ray showed a few spots.

Then he spread out the X Rays. I guess it should have been the worst day of my life but it

was actually a good day in a way, old page. The
sunlight brightened the crease of angwish that got
pressed across Fran's face as she buried it into her
arm, then pressed her arm against my shoulder
as I touched her beautiful long hair sobbing as
low and sad and soft as the soundless sound you
hear right before you score. The doctor took off
his glasses, rubbed his face, then put a finger
next to the spots. OF COURSE THERE WERE
SPOTS. I would have been a real fuckhead—a
bad fuckhead, not a good fuckhead (Crash, buddy,
I love you, you know that)—to think that there
weren't going to be spots, old page. I mean, I've
worn purpul, teel, mohve, graybrown, razberry,
and seventeen diffrent shades of red. I've spat
teeth and cracked bones and pulled ligaments in
17 states and 8 provinces over this humfrickin'
planet of ice, which I diskovered after lifting my
eyes long enough from my train set to see Glenn
Anderson swoop like a heron past four big giant
defenders and flick the puck into the net like he
was flipping a coin off the end of his thumb. The
speed, the grace, the arrowgance of the move. I
was hooked, and now, lookit, here I am in Italy.
Maybe now Fran will sleep with me. I'm not just
saying this because I'm horned up, old page. I'm

saying this because I really think I love her and now yes I want to love her inside and out, all the way. Maybe then these spots'll be for more than just dying.

THE FIVE HOLE

Because you can't see my tits and ass through my armour—and more's the pity—my Five Hole is everything: my weapon, my lure and hook, my lascivious winking eye, my love patch, my gun barrel, my tease and trick. My Five Hole has made many players hard, but even more players shrivel-dicked after squeezing the game's dark prize between my legs. My Five Hole is there; no, it's not. My Five Hole watches you sweat and work, not the other way around. My Five Hole pulls its towel back and shows you its succulent daisyhead, only to cover up like a shy girl stepping from the shower once your hands cock, tighten, then release the prize. My Five Hole is a triangle of endless space in a hot mountain of wet padding and plastic, a passageway to pure light through which the player dreams of moving as if he were a dragonfly, and it a keyhole. My Five Hole is a dark window on a moving train, a dolphin's eye, a laughing clown face that mocked you at the summer carnival when you pushed your hand up Jessica Francee's KISS ARMY T-shirt while leaning

DAVE BIDINI

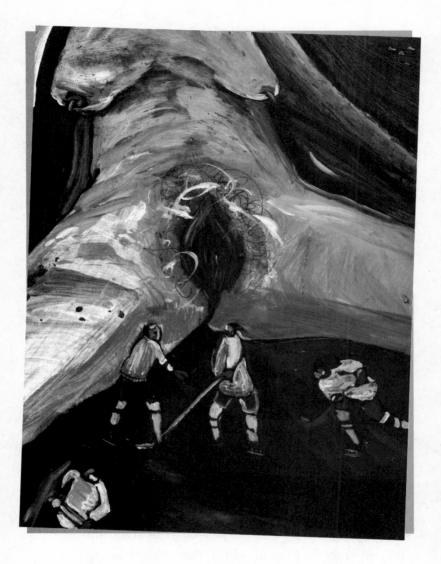

against the Spider's metal fairground struts before she turned her cheek as you came in with your tongue then laid down in the field with that guy with the caterpillar moustache and Freddie Prinze package who saw you standing there bewildered then flashed his crooked-toothed smile, which is also my Five Hole. My Five Hole is Man Ray's camera lens, Buddy Miles' bass drum. My Five Hole is the pink crux at the tip of the chameleon's tongue as it lashed out from its starving reptile's maw while Karen Shaunessy squeezed your hands squeezing the shell of her bra as she pushed you against the glass lizard enclosure of the city zoo before grabbing the back of your neck the way Rogie Vachon or Eddie Mio or Murray Bannerman did when pulling down his masks and righting his Five Hole, which was never as angry or beautiful or wild as my Five Hole, but still. My Five Hole is a silk heart pushed between salty thighs swathed in fat leather pads with their straps biting into mangrove legs covered in striped stockings gartered high on my tummy that roils with excitement as you move forward on knives riveted to boots peering through your facecage wanting to hurt me but since all pucks are chocolate and my Five Hole is insatiable you end up feeding me

DAVE BIDINI

with shots that I devour to grow stronger than any weed-dicked forward with a weakness for leather. My Five Hole has witnessed desperate men beating other men until crimson flowed heavy from their wounds, yet nothing crumples or cuts deeper than a Five Hole scorned and hot with vengeance. My Five Hole is a silver button on the waistband of the Afro-plumed Soul Train dancer who invented The Bump on ABC Saturday afternoon television as Mira Melnyk sucked on your nipples before she threw you on the cushions and ordered you to find that blinding hot square of electric flesh connected to the very middle of the brightest star in the deepest galaxy, which, coincidentally, is also my Five Hole. My Five Hole is the dangle space between Tony Esposito's hot dog bun pads and the way he was taught by the son of a son of a miner to crouch in front of shooters like he hadn't shit for days. My Five Hole is both a crooked finger coaxing you toward sporting immortality and a tattooed fist that finds you when you get there. My Five Hole is what you see when you stare across the cold damp dressing room floor swabbed with spit and ammonia, your ratty socks bundled at the ankles, and you feel small and frightened because you thought you were playing a child's game but suddenly you became overwhelmed with adult thoughts that drained the strength from your arms and knees knowing that something so terrible and forbidden existed and that you with your street hockey moves and joobie hair and aluminum shaft and feathered blade and tilted skates and parched throat and piddledick wrist shot were not worthy to occupy the same sacred patch of ice as my exultant Five Hole, which is forever mine, and never yours. Any attempt to reproduce my Five Hole in whole or in part may result in severe punishment. Unless you like that sort of thing.

ACKNOWLEDGEMENTS

Much of the blame for this story collection must be levelled at a woman named Brenda Quinn. Brenda staged a short-lived erotic reading event at the Music Gallery in Toronto in the early '90s, and two of these stories were first written for this purpose. "I am Bobby Wolf" has appeared in a slightly altered form in the *New Quarterly*. "Why I Love Wayne Bradley" was published in the *Village Voice* though at that time, Wayne had a slightly more conspicuous surname. I owe thanks to Jeff Z. Klein for pubbing the Wayne story, Brian Fawcett for writing "My Career with the Leafs," and Lorna Jackson and Darren Wershler-Henry for reading these stories. Darren was, in fact, so encouraging through this process that I stole freely from his fine book, *Apostrophe* (with Bill Kennedy), in order to create the story "The Five Hole." I would also be remiss—not to mention punched senseless—if I didn't confess that the idea for the balls salve in "I am Bobby Wolf" was harvested from the brilliant—and salacious—mind of Paul Quarrington. Further acknowledgement must go to the equally brilliant—and salacious, too, come to think of it—One Yellow Rabbit Performance Group, who adapted these stories for the stage, and to the usual suspects: Janet and the kids, my parents, DJ, M&S, Matt James, all of the folks involved with the annual Joe Burke Wolfe Island Literary Festival and, naturally, Lee and Ruth from B&G, who put these bits of tree pulp together.

Dave Bidini
PO Box 616
Station C, Toronto, ON
M6J 3R9

DAVE BIDINI's *On a Cold Road*, his popular and critically acclaimed first book about what it's like to tour Canada in a rock 'n' roll band, was published in 1998. He has since written four more books, *Tropic of Hockey* (2001), *Baseballissimo* (2004), *For Those About to Rock* (2004), and

The Best Game You Can Name (2005). When he is not writing or travelling the world, Bidini is rhythm guitarist for the Rheostatics. The band has released twelve albums to date, including *Music Inspired by the Group of Seven*, the soundtrack to the film *Whale Music* which yielded the hit song "Claire," and *The Story of Harmelodia*, a children's album. He also starred in the Gemini award-winning film *The Hockey Nomad*, as well as its sequel, *The Hockey Nomad Goes to Russia*. Dave Bidini lives in Toronto.

Other books by Dave Bidini

On a Cold Road: Tales of Adventure in
   Canadian Rock (1998)

Tropic of Hockey (2001)

Baseballissimo (2004)

For Those About to Rock (2004)

The Best Game You Can Name (2005)